Can You Catch a Mermaid?

For Clara, Elly and Joe, Ben and Rebecca,

Debbie, Louise and Mark, Barty and Camilla -

remembering our mermaid in Devon, Summer 2000

ORCHARD BOOKS

96 Leonard Street, London EC2A 4XD

Orchard Books Australia

32/45-51 Huntley Street, Alexandria, NSW 2015

ISBN 1 84121 773 5 (hardback)

ISBN 1 84121 296 2 (paperback)

First published in Great Britain in 2002

First paperback publication in 2003

Text and illustrations © Jane Ray 2002

The rights of Jane Ray to be identified as the author

and illustrator of this work has been asserted by her

in accordance with the Copyright, Designs and Patents Act, 1988.

A CIP catalogue record for this book is available from the British Library

3 5 7 9 10 8 6 4   (hardback)

3 5 7 9 10 8 6 4   (paperback)

Printed in Singapore

Can You Catch a Mermaid?

Written and illustrated by

Jane Ray

ORCHARD BOOKS

Have you ever seen a mermaid?
Have you ever seen a shimmering tail
and some strands of greeny gold hair
turning in the water?

Maybe not.

But did you know that sometimes,
just sometimes, a mermaid can turn her fishy
tail to legs and come ashore?
As long as she keeps hold of something
from her ocean home, she can return to the water.
But if she should lose that something, she is trapped on land forever.

*This is the story of Eliza,
who really did see a mermaid.*

Eliza lived with her father Tom, who was
a fisherman. Just him and her, comfortable
and close, taking care of each other.

"You are my little dolphin," he would say, holding
Eliza tight in his arms, like the harbour
walls protecting the little boats.

Eliza was shy and liked to play by herself,
searching in rock pools and collecting pebbles
and shells. Sometimes Tom worried about her.

"Why don't you go off and play with
the other children?" he would say.

But Eliza just shook her head.
"I only want to be with you," she said.

Every day, Eliza
waved goodbye to her
father as he set off in his fishing boat.

"What shall I bring you
for tea today, Little Dolphin?"
he would say. "Sardines or skate?
Hake or herring? Winkles, cockles or crab?"

And every day Eliza answered, "Can you catch a mermaid?"

One evening, as Eliza was waiting for the chug-chug-chug
of her father's boat, she saw a girl of about her own age
playing at the water's edge. They smiled at each other shyly.
The girl didn't frighten Eliza like the children at school.
Instead Eliza felt curious and wanted to talk to her.

The next morning, when Tom set off in his boat, the little girl was there again. She gave Eliza a shell that was pink and gold, and when Eliza put it to her ear it sang,

"Can I be your friend, Eliza?

Where the dolphins leap

And the sand

The girls played together all day. By the time evening came, and it was time for Eliza to go home, it felt as though they had known each other all their lives.

Come and play with me,

and the seagulls cry,

becomes the sea."

Her name was Freya and she had long greeny gold
hair and pale, pale skin. Her eyes were the colour
of stormy seas and all about her was the scent of
salt and rock pools. Around her neck she carried a
beautiful little mirror, inlaid with
pieces of coral and mother-of-pearl.

"Sing with me, Eliza," Freya called and she taught Eliza
songs so beautiful that they had to be shared.

"Dance with me, Eliza," she said and they danced together like a sea breeze.

Eliza didn't know where Freya came from or where she went to at night. Sometimes she was there and sometimes she wasn't, and then Eliza was as lonely as a sandpiper.

But one morning, Eliza found Freya crying, running up
and down at the water's edge, wringing her hands.

"I've lost my mirror. It's gone, it's gone! Oh, please help me to find it, please!
For I can't go home without it. Without it I can't ever go home!"

And then, then Eliza realised who Freya was.

Tom had told Eliza all about the mermaids,
how they can come on to the land and go
back into the sea, if they keep something
special from their ocean home with them.

Freya was a mermaid, and the little
mirror was her special thing.

Eliza took Freya's hand.

"Don't worry," she said. "We'll find your mirror."

Eliza and Freya searched all day, back and forth like beachcombers along the shoreline. But they couldn't find the mirror.

That night, Eliza took her friend home and she and Tom cared for the little mermaid as if she was their own.

Deep in the ocean, Freya's mother was looking for her daughter and, when the waves whispered the terrible news that the mirror was lost and with it her child, her grief was great and unspeakable. Her little Freya!

That night, terrible storms battered the coast where Freya was stranded.

Meanwhile, Freya stayed with Eliza
and Tom, and shared their food and their stories
and Eliza's little bed. But Freya was unhappy.

She fretted for her family and her ocean home.

Every morning she set out to search for the mirror.

Now, Eliza had a secret. A few days after Freya's arrival they were on the beach as usual, looking for the lost mirror. Eliza clambered on the rocks where the sea rushed at high tide and there she found the mirror, covered in seaweed. She washed it quickly but, instead of giving it back to Freya as she knew she should, she put it in her pocket. Eliza couldn't bear Freya to leave.

Eliza took the mirror home and hid it in her secret box. And when she was quite alone, she took it out and looked at herself in the watery glass. "I'll give it to Freya tomorrow," she thought.

But the days passed, and Eliza kept the mirror secret.

The days passed and Freya grew thinner and even paler. She no longer laughed or danced on the sand, but spent her days searching, searching, searching for the lost mirror.

The other families began to mutter about Freya.
Their catches had dwindled to almost nothing since
she had arrived and now the weather was so dark
and stormy it was dangerous to put out to sea at all.

One wild night,
Eliza couldn't sleep.
The waves crashed
against the harbour
wall. Eliza picked
up the pink and
gold shell that Freya
had given her when
they first met and
put it to her ear.
At first Eliza
heard only the
storm outside.
Then, very faintly,
she heard a
voice sighing,

"Let me go, let me go home."

Eliza looked at Freya sleeping restlessly at her side.
She knew what she must do. She crept to her
hiding place, took out the mirror, and
gently tucked it into Freya's hand.

Then she climbed back into bed
and fell into a deep sleep.

In the morning the wind had dropped. Pale
sunshine spilled into the room. Freya was gone.

Tom set sail on a calm sea. Before he left he
held Eliza extra tight. "What shall I bring
you today, my brave Little Dolphin?"

Eliza smiled a sad little smile.

But that day, Tom came back with nets full of fish.
And from then on, the village fishing nets were
always full, and Tom's was the fullest of all.

ELIZA

And that day, Eliza made new friends. Now she loves playing with the other children. They collect shells and Eliza shows them how to build mermaids out of sand.

When she puts the beautiful pink and gold shell to her ear she still hears Freya's sweet voice singing to her, and the songs she sings are of her ocean home and the silver fishes that play there.

And sometimes, in still rock pools
or in the deep green ocean,
when Eliza is out in
Tom's boat, she
thinks she
sees Freya
smiling up
at her through
the water.

Or maybe it's her own reflection.